ELMER IN THE SNOW

For Sabrina B. and Zoe Z.

A RED FOX BOOK : 0 09 972131 7

First published in Great Britain by Andersen Press Ltd 1995
Red Fox edition published 1997

9 10 8

Red Fox Books are published by Random House Children's Books,
61-63 Uxbridge Road, London W5 5SA,
a division of The Random House Group Ltd,
in Australia by Random House Australia (Pty) Ltd,
20 Alfred Street, Milsons Point, Sydney, NSW 2061, Australia
in New Zealand by Random House New Zealand Ltd,
18 Poland Road, Glenfield, Auckland 10, New Zealand
and in South Africa by Random House (Pty) Ltd,
Endulini, 5A Jubilee Road, Parktown 2193, South Africa

THE RANDOM HOUSE GROUP Limited Reg No. 954009
www.**kidsatrandomhouse**.co.uk

A CIP catalogue record for this book is available from the British Library.

Printed in China

ELMER IN THE SNOW

David McKee

RED FOX

One morning, Elmer, the patchwork elephant, met a group of elephants who didn't look very happy.

"What's the matter?" asked Elmer.

"What's the matter is that it's cold," said one of the elephants. "That's what's the matter."

"It's not really cold," said Elmer. "It's just a bit colder than usual. What you need is a good walk to warm you up. Come on, come with me."

Elmer led the elephants in a direction they didn't normally go. The way went steeply upwards and the elephants were soon puffing with the effort.

"I'm very warm now, thank you, Elmer," said one of the elephants. "Shall we go back?"

"Not yet," said Elmer. "Keep going."

After they had gone further, an elephant said,
"Elmer, look at the trees, they're different here."
"That's because we are so high up," said Elmer.
"Come on, there's something I want to show you."

A little later the elephants came out into the open and they stared at the sight—everywhere was white.

"SNOW!" they shouted. Although they had heard about snow, this was the first time they had actually seen any. The elephants rushed forward and roared with laughter as they played in the snow.

"It's really cold," called one of the elephants.

"Cold but fun," laughed another.

"Now, come and look at this," called Elmer. He was sliding on the ice of a pond that had frozen solid. One by one the others curiously joined him.

Soon the elephants were slipping and sliding and crashing and falling and really enjoying themselves. They didn't notice Elmer quietly sneak away.

The elephants forgot all about Elmer until
they heard his voice nearby.

"Help! Help! I've frozen solid."

The elephants stopped playing and hurried
to find Elmer. To their dismay, there stood a
white elephant.

"He has, he's frozen solid," gasped one of
the elephants.

Then he touched the white elephant and a piece fell off. "It's made of snow," he said.

"I know where Elmer is," chuckled another. He pointed to a line of footprints in the snow. "Come on."

The elephants followed the line of footprints but
before they reached him, Elmer appeared and with a laugh,
started throwing snowballs that he had already prepared.

It wasn't long before all the elephants were throwing snowballs at each other.

"It's starting to snow quite hard," said Elmer after a while. "It's time for us to go."

Still laughing and playing, and with the snow falling all around them, the elephants hurried back to the trees and then on home.

When they were finally home again, one of the elephants said, "Snow is fun, but it really is cold."

"Yes," said another. "It's nice to be back in the warm."

Elmer said nothing. He just smiled.